Harry and Tuck

by Holly Keller

GREENWILLOW BOOKS   New York

Watercolor paints and a black pen were used for the full-color art. The text type is Bryn Mawr Book.
Copyright © 1993 by Holly Keller. All rights reserved. No part of this book may be reproduced or utilized
in any form or by any means, electronic or mechanical, including photocopying, recording, or by any
information storage and retrieval system, without permission in writing from the Publisher.
Greenwillow Books, a division of William Morrow & Company, Inc., 1350 Avenue of the Americas,
New York, NY 10019.   Printed in Singapore by Tien Wah Press   First Edition
10 9 8 7 6 5 4 3 2 1

Library of Congress Cataloging-in-Publication Data

Keller, Holly.
Harry and Tuck / by Holly Keller.
p.   cm.
Summary: Harrison and Tucker always act and think
alike as they are growing up, but when they go to
kindergarten and end up in different classrooms
they start to develop differences.
ISBN 0-688-11462-8 (trade).   ISBN 0-688-11463-6 (lib.)
[1. Twins—Fiction.   2. Individuality—Fiction.
3. Kindergarten—Fiction.   4. Schools—Fiction.]
I. Title.   PZ7.K28132Har   1993
[E]—dc20   91-45674   CIP   AC

FOR HARRISON AND TUCKER TAYLOR,
OF COURSE!

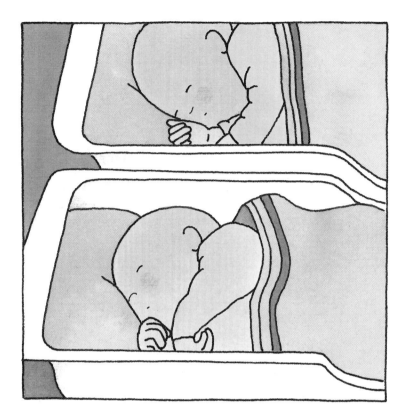

Harrison and Tucker did everything together—right from the very beginning.

Sometimes when Tucker made noises that sounded like a little song, Harrison answered with his own tune, and they understood each other perfectly.

"What kind of cereal would you like for breakfast?" Mama
asked every morning.
"I'll have wheat flakes, and Tucker wants oatmeal," Harrison
would say. Or "I'll have corn flakes, and Harrison wants Cheerios,"
Tucker would say. Because they always knew.

The day Harrison got poison ivy from playing in the woods with bare feet, Tucker said *he* itched all over.

"I see," said Papa, and he put calamine lotion on Tucker, too.

And when Tucker fell off his bicycle, Harrison cried the loudest.
"It hurts *me* here," he said, rubbing his elbow.
So Mama put Band-Aids on both of them.

Harrison could draw horses, and Tucker could draw birds,
and they both liked the color green.
"Did Harrison do this?" Miss Murphy asked Tucker at nursery
school when she saw the wall.
Tucker shook his head.
"Did Tucker do this, Harrison?" she asked.
Harrison shook his head.
Miss Murphy frowned and gave them each a soapy sponge,
so they could wash the wall—together.

But when Tucker ate all of Harrison's popcorn, Harrison was mad.
So mad that he jumped out of the bushes to scare Tucker. And Katie,
who lived next door, *really* got scared.

"Tucker did it," Harrison told Papa when Katie's mama
  called on the telephone.
"Harrison did it," Tucker insisted, and Papa groaned.
"Off to bed now, you two," Mama scolded.

In the morning Mama opened the bedroom window. The sky
was very blue, and the air was cool.
"Just right for the first day of kindergarten," she said.

Harrison chose a red shirt, and Tucker chose a red shirt, and they both had new sneakers and yellow socks.

"I hope we don't get that mean teacher with the funny hair," Tucker
said to Harrison as they walked to school.
"Yeah," Harrison said, "Me, too."

"Good morning," said Mrs. Beech, who was greeting all the new
   kindergarteners.
"Harrison, you will be in my class, and Tucker will be with Mr. Stone."

Harrison moved closer to Tucker, and Tucker took his hand.
"What will I do if my sneakers come untied?" he whispered.
"Who will tickle me if I cry?" Tucker asked, wondering if he
might be just about to.

Harrison thought about Tucker most of the morning.
And Mr. Stone let Tucker look through the glass in Mrs. Beech's
door just to be sure Harrison was all right.

"Goodbye, Tuck," Mr. Stone called from the door when it was time to go home.
"See you tomorrow, Harry," Mrs. Beech said cheerfully.

Harrison and Tucker looked at each other.

"Harry?" Tucker said.

"Tuck?" Harry said.

And they started laughing and talking at the same time.

"I had apple juice and chocolate cookies."

"I had lemonade and peanut butter crackers."

"I played kickball."

"I used the hammer."

"There's a girl in my class named Isabel," Tucker said. "She's really nice."

"Nicky is in my class," Harrison said, "and he knows a lot about rockets."

"Did you like it?" Tucker asked.

Harrison nodded his head.

"Me, too," Tucker said, "but I wished you were there."

When they got home, Tucker ran across the yard.
"Come on," he called. "Let's climb the apple tree!"
Harrison sang a little song. Tucker hummed an answer.
And they giggled, because they understood.

The next day Harrison wore a striped shirt and blue socks, and Tucker wore a yellow shirt with red socks.

"Have a happy day, boys," Papa said when he kissed them good-bye.

"See you later, Harry," Tucker said when they got to
Mr. Stone's door.
"See you later, Tuck," Harrison answered, and he turned
to go down the hall.